Monster in the Garden

First published 2009
Evans Brothers Limited
2A Portman Mansions
Chiltern Street
London W1U 6NR

British Library Cataloguing in Publication Data

Rooney, Anne.
  Monster in the Garden -- (Spirals)
  1. Children's stories.
  I. Title II. Series

  823.9'2-dc22

ISBN-13: 978 0 237 53883 5 (hb)
ISBN-13: 978 0 237 53889 7 (pb)

Printed in China

Editor: Louise John
Design: Robert Walster
Production: Jenny Mulvanny

Monster in the Garden

Anne Rooney
and Bruno Robert

Evans

Patrick heard something in the garden.
It sounded a bit like a cat.

"Mieuw, mieuw."

But Patrick didn't have a cat. And
the family next door didn't have a
cat either.

"Mieuw,
mieuw."

The noise came from high up in a tree.
Patrick looked up but he could only see
green leaves.

"Lunch, Patrick!" called Mum,
bringing a sandwich outside.

Mum put the plate on the grass and
Patrick began to read his comic.

A few minutes later, Patrick looked
up and went to take a bite, but the
sandwich had gone!

Cats don't eat sandwiches, he thought.
But there was that noise again.
"Mieuw, mieuw."

Patrick saw a flash of blue in the bushes.

Cats aren't blue, he thought.

Patrick went into the kitchen.

"What's blue and goes 'mieuw' and eats sandwiches?" he asked.

"I don't know, Patrick. What is blue and goes 'mieuw' and eats sandwiches?"

"No, it's not a joke!" said Patrick.
"There's one outside."

Patrick took another sandwich. This time he held it in his hand. He read his comic and waited.

Nothing happened.

Suddenly, he felt something tugging on his sandwich. He looked up just in time to see a trail of eyes disappear into the bushes. One, two, three, four, five golden eyes!

Patrick ran inside.

"There's a blue monster with loads of eyes that says 'mieuw' and eats sandwiches and it's in the garden," he said, without stopping for breath.

"That's nice, dear," said Mum. "Why don't you go and catch it?"

Patrick had never caught a monster before. It didn't sound safe. What if it ate boys as well as sandwiches? Perhaps it had sharp claws and pointy teeth?

Maybe it could breathe fire or turn him to stone with its five eyes?

He armed himself for the monster hunt.

Patrick waited and waited.

"Mieuw, mieuw," went the monster.
It was in a tree. Patrick looked up.

He could see blue between the leaves.
He could see five big, golden staring
eyes that never blinked.

"If I'm going to catch a monster, I need to make a trap," he said.

He took a basket and some string. He took Mum's dressing gown, made some more sandwiches and, finally, he laid out his monster trap.

Then he hid in a bush and waited.

And waited...

21

With a flash of blue and green, and a loud clatter of wings, the monster swooped on the sandwiches.

Clonk!

The monster was in the basket. It struggled and squawked.

"Mieuw, mieuw!"

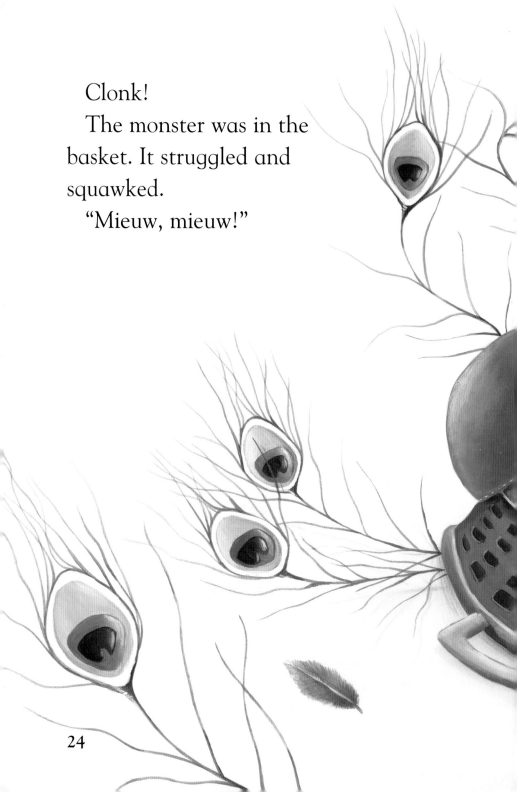

Patrick bundled the monster into the dressing gown and tied it with the belt. He took the monster parcel into the house. It wasn't easy!

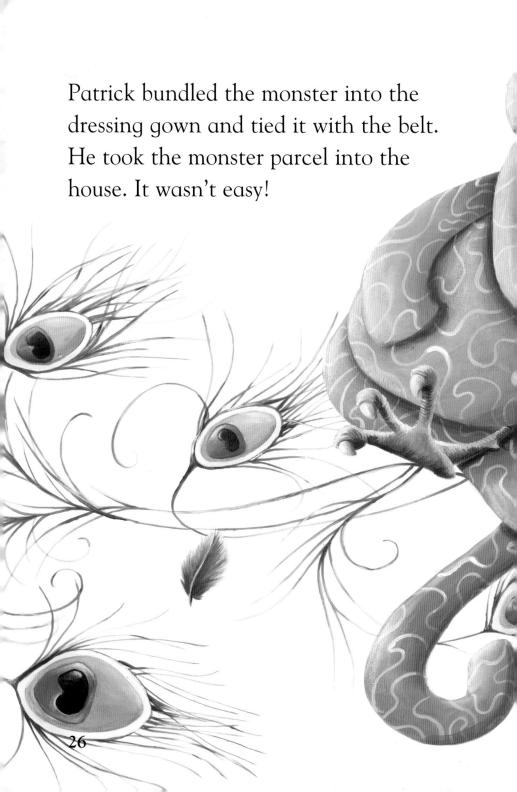

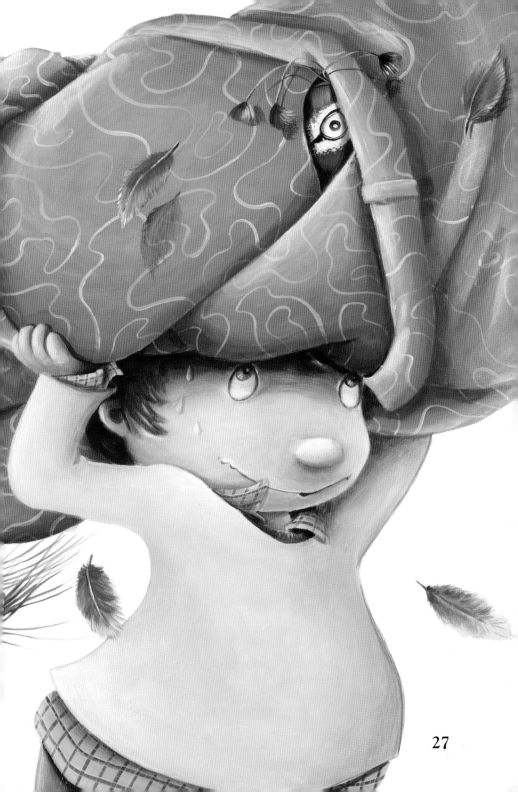

Mum was watching the news.

The monster squawked again.

"Mieuw, mieuw!"

"Patrick, look!" cried Mum, pointing to the TV screen. "You've found the lost peacock!"

Patrick held the monster tight, while Mum ran to phone the wildlife park.

Two men arrived in a large van from the wildlife park. They unwrapped the monster gently and put it in a crate.

"Does he have to go?" asked Patrick. "Can't I keep him?"

"Take this ticket," said one of the men, "you can come to see him any time you like."

"I will," laughed Patrick, "as long as he doesn't eat my sandwiches again!"

Why not try reading another **Spirals** book?

Megan's Tick Tock Rocket by Andrew Fusek Peters, Polly Peters
HB: 978 0237 53348 0 PB: 978 0237 53342 7

Growl! by Vivian French
HB: 978 0237 53351 0 PB: 978 0237 53345 8

John and the River Monster by Paul Harrison
HB: 978 0237 53350 2 PB: 978 0237 53344 1

Froggy Went a Hopping by Alan Durant
HB: 978 0237 53352 9 PB: 978 0237 53346 5

Amy's Slippers by Mary Chapman
HB: 978 0237 53353 3 PB: 978 0237 53347 2

The Flamingo Who Forgot by Alan Durant
HB: 978 0237 53349 6 PB: 978 0237 53343 4

Glub! by Penny Little
HB: 978 0237 53462 2 PB: 978 0237 53461 5

The Grumpy Queen by Valerie Wilding
HB: 978 0237 53460 8 PB: 978 0237 53459 2

Happy by Mara Bergman
HB: 978 0237 53532 2 PB: 978 0237 53536 0

Sink or Swim by Dereen Taylor
HB: 978 0237 53531 5 PB: 978 0237 53535 3

Sophie's Timepiece by Mary Chapman
HB: 978 0237 53530 8 PB: 978 0237 53534 6

The Perfect Prince by Paul Harrison
HB: 978 0237 53533 9 PB: 978 0237 53537 7

Tuva by Mick Gowar
HB: 978 0237 53879 8 PB: 978 0237 53885 9

Wait a Minute, Ruby! by Mary Chapman
HB: 978 0237 53882 8 PB: 978 0237 53888 0

George and the Dragonfly by Andy Blackford
HB: 978 0237 53878 1 PB: 978 0237 53884 2

Monster in the Garden by Anne Rooney
HB: 978 0237 53883 5 PB: 978 0237 53889 7

Just Custard by Joe Hackett
HB: 978 0237 53881 1 PB: 978 0237 53887 3

The King of Kites by Judith Heneghan
HB: 978 0237 53880 4 PB: 978 0237 53886 6